ALSO BY JAMES L. HARTER SR.

Mindsongs: Chapter One

Heartfelt Thoughts: Chapters Two & Three
Mindsongs/Treks
Mindsongs/Strolling

Heartfelt Thoughts: Chapters Four & Five
Mindsongs/Wayfarer
Lifesongs

Heartfelt Thoughts: Chapters Six & Seven
Preface to Life
Life Goes on

Heartfelt Thoughts

Chapters Eight and Nine

James L. Harter Sr.

Heartfelt Thoughts Chapters Eight and Nine by James L. Harter Sr.
Copyright © 2014 by James L. Harter Sr.

Cover design and layout by ClearView Press Inc

Heartfelt Thoughts Chapters Eight & Nine by James L. Harter Sr.
116p. ill. cm.
ISBN 978-1-935795-29-2

ClearView Press, Inc.
PO Box 353431
Palm Coast, FL 32135-3431
www.clearviewpressinc.com

Printed in the United States of America

To my inner child.

And, to my dear wife, Shirley

A child within me gifts a smile

I pause to glimpse and chat awhile

Contents

Chapter Eight: *Glimpses of Life*

Chapter Eight:
Glimpses of Life

Preface

Glimpsing into my self, my life, as I have been doing through my poetic sense; I have gleaned new insight into my being. In wonder, I have discovered what I think I am. I am so awestruck and so ecstatic, for I have discovered on my own, the very same things that others have spoken about in their voluminous how to books. I cannot begin to relate to you the joy I feel. Even my poetic sense is speechless.

Glimpsing into my self, my life, I have talked to my inner child, without fully realizing he was actually my Inner Child. Not until I excerpted thoughts and discussions from John Bradshaw's book, "Homecoming", did I fully comprehend my self revelations.

Glimpsing into my self, my life, I have felt a regeneration emerging in my Now. And now, many of my previous writings which appeared enigmatic to me to this point in time; have now taken on a new meaning. The puzzle is coming together.

Glimpsing into my self, my life, I will now do so with new fervor, new enthusiasm, new playfulness, new spontaneity, and an extended, but new wonder. I endear and embrace my Child and welcome his truth. Seeking takes on a new challenge, discovery – a new thrill, and fulfillment – a new goal.

As I glimpse, so may you.

As I may do, so may you.

One Small Step for Man

A glance, askance, and a shadow wisps
I hark to sounds and my heart jump shifts
I chance to tread and I brave to enter
I turn to self, towards my epicenter
A child within me gifts a smile
I pause to glimpse and I chat awhile
I step into a world brand new
My universe has a glorious view

The Inevitability of Being Me

'tis a foregone conclusion that if I am

then, in a sense, I am

but I need to have the sense to know

that, indeed, I am

a life could be living and dying unknowing

not even knowing the essence of his being

the wandering soul is lost 'til another time

'til another place, - another space

thank you, my soul for sharing me with you

thank you for giving me your insight

I am indebted to your welfare

To the inevitability of being with you

Sun of Man

reach on out and touch the sun

on this clear, crisp Christmas Day

the still is broken only by occasional quivers

the peace that lies without, also rests within

yet under this same sun lies unrest

tensions in a land where once a child was blessed

reach on out and touch this sun

on this clear, crisp Christmas Day

perhaps many quivers from the peace within

will come to rest in the land that is without

what a revolting development this is
the bulldozer creeping o'er the meadow
scooping the earth, upending the ant herds
sending wheat shards into turmoil
scattering redwings
screeching for new sky
What of the meadow mice?
Did the rabbit get away?
What from yonder meadow rises?
fracturing the placid sky
a building I designed will soon be born
the bulldozer creeping o'er the meadow
grunting through the drifting dust
pushing rich topsoil into a lifeless dome
golden helmeted ant men feverishly laboring
begin to build my dream hill, my monolith
my towering pinnacle
my habitat for humankind
I used to walk this meadow
Did I have it do this?
Was there some other way?
the queen is so demanding, the colony keeps growing
I am but a worker tending to her whims
I used to walk this meadow
How many more will she take away?

Yours for the Asking

if I had an answer for everything
I would have no reason to question anything
but the fun is in the asking
even if there are no answers
some day, someone will have an answer
and I'll be glad I had asked the question

When you are alone and your stroll through the forest
seeking some solace or an unknown event that might
occur; discovery of something thrills the heart and mind
like nothing else can.
This is when Raynondskill emerges.

Raymondskill Falling

I had been told of Raymondskill
When I enter the forest,
I hear him rushing
in the quiet of the forest
I hear him gushing
and my ears lead me onward,
onward to Raymondskill

My feet step gently
as I advance on clouds
of needle down and leaf pillow
Anticipation of what I am not sure, but
exhilarated anticipation is the lure
a path, takes me closer and lower, louder he becomes
I cannot wait, I utter;
I cannot wait for Raymondskill

A spring rivulet is my stepping lane
I slip; almost overturn an ankle, and all alone
whew, that was close. *Slow down*, I said
he will be there when you get there
as always Raymondskill.

(continues)

Then the coolness comes,
and I am drawn by the freshness
the scene explodes before me
and there in instant,
falls Raymondskill

Swirling mist and power
Oh, the feeling power,
A world is rushing to me
and carrying me
plunging me with him
I swoon;
almost believing I am part of the power
In awe I stand, all alone, I and the power
All alone with Raymondskill

The trees, the moss, the rocks,
the sky, and I, all alone.
We live the thrill with Raymondskill

Field of Dreams

When I was a kid,

    Fields were alive
    with goldenrods and milkweed pods
    stinging nettles and sticky burrs
    Fields were just fields
    neither used or abused
    Meadow mice made matt-mounded nests
    pheasant and rabbit wandered at will
    right before my eyes
    in the city
    in front of our home
    all free to roam

When I was a kid,

    We picked the sticky burrs
    sticking them together – sticky bricks
    making little sticky houses
    or making sticky balls
    today's Velcro, sticking to our clothes
    Stay away from the stinging nettle
    It would itch like crazy
    And stay away from Brer' Rabbit's
    briar bramble barbs
    slashing skin
    sending self to shelf
    for iodine and band-aids

(continues)

When I was a kid,

    The white blood of the milkweed
    oozed, making fingers so icky
    In the fall, we used to pick the pods
    and blow the seed to the air
    watching the frilly parachutes
    snagging on late summer's weeds
    or sailing out of sight
    breeze bobbing on their merry way

When I was a kid,

    We used to run and play tag or hide and seek
    among the dense meadow grasses
    or we just used to run for the fun of running
    I felt a freedom seldom since felt
    an abandonment so difficult to describe
    We used to roll and frolic
    in the meadow grass oases
    creating matted trails
    crawling about, giggling gleefully

When I was a kid,

        I could go to the innards of my friendly field
        I could lie down
        and hide from the people world
        I could listen to field sounds
        and wait and watch for crawly things
        I could just lie and dream
        I could feel the field and
        I felt the field feeling me

Sylvan Serenade

On a crisply cold one wintry day
under a clear blue-perfect sky
I felt the touch of an old warm friend
catching the glint in his golden eye
He bade me to trek to the ends of time
always bringing me back once more
then leading me out to a sylvan spot
to hark to a symphonious score
Tingles of sounds that touch my heart
and the sights that embrace my eyes
sends the chords of screaming silence
dancing off to resounding highs
Wind harps stringing thru the barren branches
shards of silver shimmering in blinking shine
woodwinds playing with swaying needle reeds
thumping clumps of snow freeing boughs of pine
Sounds of sights continue whether I am or I am not
'tis for me to be aware of what this life does bring

(continues)

all the symphonies and serenades sung in sense-around

must reach my deepest part for all this to mean

something

I was led here to savor this sylvan serenade

and to hold court with my inner self worth

to witness the song of all that is judged

by a Master giving life to eternal rebirth

Some Quatrains that come to Mind

Q-1
I walk to the center
    of all that is the beginning
And the end of the past
    opens to all that is revealing

Q-2
If I make my own bed,
    who remains to cover me?
If I fall fast asleep,
    who will ever tuck me in?

Q-3
I see sin, not as enemy
    who becomes my friend
But as a friend
    who forgets me quickly   (continues)

Q-4
Life's mirror has great depth
      in perception and reflection
A true friend cannot know of me
      unless I know of him in return

Q-5
I see love indescribably in:
      birdsong, moon glow,
            morning dew, wind blow,
                  the edge of a tear, and you

Q-6
My foolish heart blurts forth
      in a gushing multi-syllable
The wisest soul best remains
      in silence, forever forgivable

Let me be

let me be
let me go to the shadows of my dreams
let me seek the light of understanding
let me forever be in my presence
let me know myself for what I am
let me be

The Wait

I turn my face upwards

to the sky

I wait

for the rain to come

to dance on my face

I wait

to cleanse my heart

with the freshness

yet no rain falls

still, I wait

and then it comes

the unseen

the unfelt

soothes my lips

and the wait

was worth it

Nothing but a Waiting Game

He said not to try so gosh darn hard
to take it easy, be patient and don't blow it
the words will come to you and when they do
they'll be right and you will darn well know it
remember that
the deepest and truest feelings create the poet

telepathic thoughts are floating all around you
all you have to do is reach out and catch 'em
a flurry of words pours swiftly from your mind
compose, organize, construct, rime and match 'em
remember that
a hen who's patient with her eggs will hatch 'em

Listen to your mind and the body will follow

Nothing is wrenching in my mind
There's no feeling of deep morose
Nothing is tearing the heart apart
Nothing's festering in the throes
A mind in turmoil has a lot to explore
A lot to express, a lot to lament about
A wrenching mind screams out for help
Wallowing in overwhelming self-doubt
Thoughts that emerge from the depths
Of this troubled and hobbled heart
Bare forth their emotions and truths
As their world comes quickly apart
But once they have stepped from the fire
Sending all of their demons to flight
Their joys in hearts and songs in minds
Are bright balloons soaring into the light

to my inner self, I say

if I am here, where are you
'in the absence of presence"
if you are here, where am I
"in the presence of absence"

A Love – That Love

there is this place I can't imagine
a place where colors have no hue
a place where I see a light so dimly
a place to go when I am blue
yet there is no hate to feel or borrow
no thoughts to send the heart to burn
no daggers to pierce my eyes so fiercely
no poison to make my stomach turn

there is a love I need not imagine
a love that receives the cupid dart
a love that takes my soul completely
a love that quicks me from the start
I accept that love and before tomorrow
that love will blossom, as it glows
that love will unfold each petal boldly
that love will be my crimson rose

I get so fed up and incensed with my architectural peers when they tend to believe that the absurd, destructive designs are worthy of awards. Even the mentioning and raving how wonderful these maniacal structures are, does not rest well with me. The likes of Graves, Eisenman, and Tigerman disgust me enough. But when peers such as Gehry and Johnson get on the bandwagon, just to be with it, I sense a foreboding future for the architect. Society deserves to be treated better.

Architecture, in my estimation, should not be as whimsical as these designers purport. Where is the integrity of the critics? Can't they see that this shock valued architecture is feeding the ego of the designers? The critics swallow all the rhetoric and gibberish of the maniac, nodding exuberantly and grunting in accord. The maniac blurts on while laughing all the way to the bank.

Architecting Nonsense - Architecting Shame

If I speak in gibberish
the grunts do think me wise
and no matter what I say or do
I'm the greatest in their eyes
If I design in gibberish
the grunts do gape in awe
and no matter what I say or do
they think I bear no flaw
The architect of gibberish
is a fool who grunts adore
and no matter what I say or do
they listen only to the whore

Hand-wrought

he created it himself from scratch
the hand of time sculpted scrapers to the sky
but I thought I could do more
so I bore my heart to the sun,
and I molded the stars in my dreams
I screamed at the moon
I talked to the trees
And, as I was soothed
by the swirling, shifting sea
the structure emerged from within
and, in its image, I saw me

The Far Pavilions

in the silence of a dream
the image emerged
and surged forward as a star shot
the brilliancy of the design
brought the far horizon into reality
reflections of the image
outshined the horizons past
moments of ecstasy were born
in the silence of a dream

River Run

       from the edge of a ledge
amidst the pines and moss
       there in the deep below
at the very, very bottom
       the serpents rage
and wriggle and roar
       peering into the writhing pit
vertigo at my nerve tips
       the surge of the torrent
holds my soul in rapture
       tormenting and teasing
squeezing eyes breathless
       sending tingles into joy bumps
       on and on, forever, on and on
quicksilver slithers repeat
       yet each frame unique
and on and on she flows
       the swirls and coiling twirls
trysting with my soul
       the water-down takes me along
a cool liquid refreshment
       going with the flow
letting it take me wherever
       letting it cleanse my soul

I love this time.

Insight

thru a picture window clearly

changing scenery comes and goes

am I a player, or am I merely

cheering from the highest rows

Hindsight

it's so simple to reset the timer

recreating what I could have done

if I'm to be a mountain climber

I'd better finish what I've begun

Foresight

if I had the foresight

to see what I've seen

I'd lay back and relax

with no reason to dream

for no matter what happens

what's been said, has been said

and in a life of no mystery

I, just as well, should drop dead

write on

write on, ye gallant poets, write on
write on ye word warriors
ye mighty wielders of the pen
ye vendors of verse
write on ye renderers of rhyme
thy quill is like blades of reeds
all their edges cut with ease
so write on ye men of great measure
remember all thy dreams
and write on

Here and Now

a larkspur, languid and lonely
drooping in the dreary lea
rallies from its sorry state
prides it blue,   challenges the skies
screams o'er the other dweller's cries
"here I am; here am I"
blue eyes shining, "here I am, am I"
"I am a larkspur and I am here; am I "

Not so; "Silly Putty"

there lays
a slimy clump of graying goop
a dormant, silent hunch-backed droop
until a foot slowly pumps the waiting treadle
the wheel rotates quietly
hands deft, fingers nimble
in the silence of the turn
evolves a graceful urn
a heart directs a talent to feel
as it molds the art
on the potter's wheel
beauty that comes from a lump so lifeless
is so very, very priceless

Feeling Free

I go now, for I know now.
The sands of yester-time shall beckon me once more;
receiving echo memories from a far off distant shore.
come back to me
remember me
dimpled tot with curly lock
come back to me
remember how we used to be
remember me
we were free
the child you see
is your echo, your memory
remember me
come back to me
come with me
I go now, for I know now
Sands of yester-time from a far off distant shore;
sending echo memories to my ever-minding door.
Come with me; I feel free
I know it's not just who I am,
Or what I am, or who I'll be
I know full well when I spread my wings
Feeling free, feeling so free
Knowing I am finally, finally me
Knowing I will be finally, finally free

Praise

when I close my weary eyes tonight
and honor the Holy Trinity
I'll think of all the men who fight
Far across the broadening sea
And all they do to keep freedom right
Just for you, and you, and me

Cover-up

there was a time, you need not ask

a time when all the world did sing

when it was fun just remembering

as busy hands took the time to task

the future became the coming thing

no yester thoughts stood lingering

each soul backed its carefree mask

View from the Bridge

I return to the river run still rampant
Savoring snowy scenes salves the senses
Falling flurry feathers fill my focused frame
White sky wizards speckle the spectacle
I've never had a feeling quite like this before
If I did, it's better than it ever was before
I'll take more, I do implore; please give me more
I could spend my life watching you
I could live my time here with you
But I must leave you now
I make unto you this solemn vow
Save me for another day
I will pass again this way

Something Worth Thinking About

who is over my shoulder   hovering about
sending seeds to soul   ready to sprout

whose hands are these   holding the light
guiding the quill   held poised to write

whose thoughts are these   my eyes now see
emerging from the well of an astounded me

is it heaven's friends   or my child inside
is it my conscience free   or a self confide

in any event   the thrill of mind's eye
is the best therapy   that no money can buy

You know me

A voice on the very edge
of this waking dawn
spoke to me and said
"You know me."
It was so clear for me to hear
It seemed as a dream; yet not
Seeking a source, I found none
Except maybe one
Now the search has just begun

Bookmarks from The Past

On the nearby shelves, a reach and a half away

Mother's many books of muse beckoned yesterday

There, pressed between the pages of her collection

Lay moments of her time, tokens of her reflection

Torn paper snips and rusty paper clips

Ribbons of satin and strands of yarn

Postcard, postage stamps and postscripts

News clippings and notes for speeches

Empty envelopes with lots of doodles

Scraps of almost anything and everything

And most of all

Leaves, dried and fragile

Sassafras, witch hazel

Birch, oak, and maple

Leaves, placed in reverence next to a beloved rhyme

Leaves, pressed in her lifetime and revered in mine

Why   Wait   Fly

you reach on high

you touch the sky

you see the heavens

and you wonder why

there's war and there's hate

and beliefs testing state

adultery seeks no reason

and your soul can't wait

to reach up for the high

and to touch the sky

to seek the heavens

and into the wonderment fly

And here it is said another way:

Her Majesty's Secret Service

Did you see the moon last night?

I did; - over my left shoulder too.

Her star spangled cloak

Was spread o'er the earth

A protecting mantle.

She vainly preened her tresses

In the calm, still waters

Of a great and wondrous lake

Now and then, she impatiently

Brushed aside a wandering cloud

Obscuring her beauty

One wonders how common men

In witness of so much majesty

Still fight and kill, - a travesty

Here also is a bookmark found with a poem written
anonymously.

Whatever is, - is Best

I know as my life grows older

And mine eyes have clearer sight

That under each rank wrong somewhere

There lies the root of right

That each sorrow has its purpose

By the sorrowing oft un-guessed

But as sure as the sun brings morning

Whatever is, - is best

I know that each sinful action

As sure as the night brings shade

Is sometimes somewhere punished

Though the hour be long delayed

I know that the soul is aided

Sometimes by the heart's unrest

And to grow means oft to suffer

But whatever is, - is best

(continues)

I know there are no errors

In the great eternal plan

And all things work together

For the final good of man

And I know when my soul speeds onward

In the great eternal quest

I shall say as I look backward

Whatever is, - is best

Beatitudes

Blessed are the eyes of a wholesome soul

who spies the doughnut after he sees the hole.

Blessed is he

who understands a tree

Blessed is the one

who's life has just begun

Presence of Mind

A gift to myself would certainly be

understanding the child abiding in me

to walk and to talk and to ultimately find

that my child here within me is my presence of mind

Windows of Time

'Tis times like these
when my windows of love
open to absorb the freshness of you
and as the blossom
of the crimson rose
unfolds its petals
for me to savor the essence of you

So 'tis the time
when my heart's sunbeams
dance within the radiance of you
and as the undying spirit
of my universal soul
melds freedom
with caring into a oneness with you

Sticks and Stones

When the acid nib of a poison pen
sends searing sneering slivers
desecrating life and degrading men.
Then the wrath his quill delivers
stays in the caverns of his own den
tormenting his raging rivers

A Froggie Would a Wooing Go

in the greenie fronds 'midst the weedie bogs
while in a southern sultry slumber time of day
'round the lillie ponds pumped the bellie frogs
belching and croaking the piercing night away
on this eve of wedding wands
                         'midst clinks of frothy grogs
two loves were toasted by a horde of friends and kin

but 'twas the bellie frogs from the weedie bogs
who stole the night drowning out the people din
seems the bellie frogs 'midst the lillie ponds
had their own boasting and toasting time to do
and from the weedie bogs
                         'midst the greenie fronds
all the loves and lovers emerged to sing and woo

If you want to

make some sense,

try coining some words,

send yourself

to the ends of yourself and go.

And where it leads

will be insight to your own destiny.

Wit's End

on the edge he stood

letting cool water fingers

play with his toes

and in so doing

his woes

went

Why are people oh so wimpy?

Where's their guts?

Intestinal Fortitude

I stood my ground today

And in so doing

I upheld my credo

And was applauded

for my fortitude

not for the laurels gestured

but for the principles

justified

Love-star

I want to be your morning sun

To kiss awake your shielded eyes

To touch you with the warmth I harbor

To brighten up your clouded skies

Now as the blush of day turns golden

And invigorating feelings heighten

May all the love I offer freely

Embrace your heart, infill, enlighten

I am your daystar burning brightly

A radiant eye all dressed in blue

With beams of sparkle, joy and comfort

And sanctum strength to pull you through

Tho' old sol bows in wondrous splendor

Preparing another newborn day

Love will last beyond each morrow

And within your soul forever stay

Write Rhyme, Wrong Time

fingers on the keyboard
fingers poised for flight
anticipating, ever waiting
what tho'ts of mine tonight
these days of falling splendor
prods heart to seek and share
the words of verse lay dormant
as a tree whose limbs are bare

fingers on the keyboard
fingers poised for flight
anticipating, ever waiting
grasping searchingly for light
I fear I've lost my poetic art
hope my mind is playing possum
I need a jolt, a thunderbolt
to crack the seeds to blossom

fingers on the keyboard
fingers poised for flight
anticipating, ever waiting
I've yet to start to write
the verse appears so trivial
when it's wrong writing time
pure unadulterated frustration
waiting for a misplaced rhythm

A Gift of God

I escape to where I know not.

I go to the abyss of my destiny

and find only an enigma.

What am I living for?

What is my reason for being?

Why need a soul learn?

To see a miracle

I look only to myself

To be a miracle

I look beyond myself

For I am my own destiny

I believe that I am what I am

My life is God's gift to me

My fulfillment is my gift to God.

Only the lonely

somewhere hidden in this debris
he must be
a haggard fetus
a shivering lump
who wallows thru hollow hours
each desolate day the same
who sends silhouetted monologues
off pace
out of place
who burns cardboard castles
in rusted drums
whose naked fanning fingers
are licked by forgotten flickers
whose sullen, barren eyes
stare ahead, wanton, dead
sparks of life dwindle
along with the waning fire
old castles   cold ashes
cold comes then, once again
wandering on
to yet another dingy shadow
leaving none to wonder
none to care
leaving nothing to share
not even a void
his empty dreams must be
hidden in this debris somewhere

Ponderings

1

a time to ponder
a time to wonder
then the beginning
now, not far at hand
is, as in the beginning
a time to understand

2

I am blind if my insight has not eyes to see
As I wonder, new understanding will come to me

3

each day is a wonder
each day is a treat
so long as I wonder
then so shall I eat

4

the past has lost its wonder
there lies no mystery
I am of the future now
For there is where I'll be

Here are three more writings performed in the Japanese haiku style:

Creature Comforts

warm breezes snuggling

relishing the entrapment

in each other's hearts . . .

**

sitting by the hearth

as fireflies flash dance upward

shadows gain wisdom . . .

**

in his comfort zone

the creature sulked contented

hiding memories . . .

Fallen Angel Rising

did you think

that I would ever change

to be molded in your image

or be sculpted by your whims

to be a puppet

on a fragile string, dangling

manipulative?   brainless?

I will not give you that satisfaction.

my strength is in my heartfelt hands.

my destiny is mine alone.

I am my own creator

for I play the lead.

take heed. I cast thee out.

so stay away.

go direct someone else's one act play.

he may have a goal but what a poor soul.

Hark and ye shall listen.
                    Seek and ye shall find.

the little cricket sitting in the forest meadow
vainly jumped in search of a friendly fellow
he rubbed his legs together
sending out his staccato calling
but there were no ears wherein
his cry would e'er be falling

he wept and wept, and his sadness grew and grew
until the tears he shed, became the morning dew
when you trek upon the forest floor
and roam from glen to thicket
remember to hark for the sounds
especially, the lonesome cricket

when you see the morning dew weeping everywhere
please do this little task for him, if you really care
peer deep into the teardrop
real hard, and you just might
catch the sparkle in his eye
when his dark becomes his light

Ménage à trois

Here we are together, alone.
I know. It is so peaceful.
I love peacefulness.
Me too.
And I love to be with you.
Me too.
And I love you.
Me too.
Me too what?
I love me too.
You mean "You love me too."
That is what I said.
You have not said, "I love you."
I do.
You do what?
I do love to be with me and you.
I do love me as I love you.
We are here together all alone.
All is so very peaceful.
I do love it so.
Sigh.
Me too.
Who said that?
Me.
Me too.

The Gap

in the whispers of my mind
I hear breathtaking thoughts
only to get them to speak
to scream unto this paper
to share me with you
so let us build a bridge
one where I can freely prance
from reality to fantasy
and back again
I'll urge
all the children
in my mind
to help me bridge the gap
and then, perhaps, some day
It'll take our breaths away

If you're happy and you know it, Clap Your Hands

just as a fly up on the ceiling
stands there upside down
I will sometimes wonder
if I'm the hero or the clown
we get hung up with strife and glory
forgetting all the joy on this earth
keep savoring the age-old story
know what true happiness is worth

He said," Suffer the little children to come unto me."

Now I think I know what He meant.

The Child Inside

the imagination of the mind

is as spring, all fresh

blossoming anew

bursting with energy

exploding with joy

the imagination of the mind

is a cherub in constant awe

touching, exploring

seeking, finding

insatiably curious

accept and doubt, shout out

act silly without regret

live, think young

let your cares go

dare to challenge

imagine how much you can achieve

if besides all that you believe

you let the child in you conceive

Wilfred J. Funk , poet. Lexicographer and President of Funk and Wagnall's Publishing Company; once listed what he considered to be the ten most beautiful words in the English language. These words he stated were chosen because they were: *". . . beautiful in meaning and in the musical arrangement of their letters . . ."*

His list was compiled after he thoroughly sifted through thousands of words. The words he chose were: chimes, dawn, golden, hush, lullaby, luminous, melody, mist, murmuring and tranquil. Without being funky, let's try our hand in putting them all into a verse of some kind . . .

By Dawn's Early Light

the hush of dawn kissed
the murmuring tranquil mist goodbye
as the luminous sun-chimes
danced in the golden melody
of its silent lullaby

Self Proclamation

I say to myself
what a wonderful day
a day to reflect
to believe in my being
to sing in my heart
to dream a new dream
I say to myself
what a beautiful day

all calm and serene
my spirit runs free
the songs in my heart
within mine eyes gleam

Lazarus

the bard . . slumped over . . like a lump of lard . . I
caught him startling off guard . . he snapped erect . .
trying to protect the solitude of his soul . . .I stole his
dream . . buried . . overburdened . . imprisoned by fear.
He burst forth . . blossoming . . rhythmic chimes soaring
. . fingertips imagining the verse . . penned freely . .
deliberately . . beautifully . . truthfully . . he challenges
his soul . .to pursue other dreams . . from within

Love is in The Air

tossing my child high above me
split second sharing
eyes meeting eyes
squeals of surprise
giggles of joy
spontaneous love
and an endearing trust
seen in those
smiling pools of blue
and then I caught him
and I hugged him

    I am so ensconced in thought trying to recall if I was
ever tossed like a ball or ever shared that kind of moment with
my Dad. Will any of my sons remember that moment from
their pasts?

Soul Baring

Wearing no shoes
bought, begged or borrowed
I go
barefooted
I tread onward
across the sands of my time
the souls of my feet
feel the grit of life
My toes
embrace
the quicksilver
fingers of temptation
My skin
relentlessly wrestles
with the changing gusts
of desire and torment
My nostrils
flare with the
exhilarating breath of life
My eyes
view the vastness
of my soul's elixir
My ears
partake my heart's
pounding waves
My footprints
before me are childlike
greeting each step
with great joy
I tread on and on
trying to catch up with my child

The Beginning

. . . I tread on and on

trying to catch up with my child

Chapter Nine:
Catching Up

. . . I tread on and on
trying to catch up with my child

Preface

If I had an inkling of what my next poem would be, I wouldn't be writing these words I happen to be writing right at this very moment.

Poetry is so spontaneous. Poetry is so emotionally and spiritually dependent that the true poet dares not contrive or compose or force his subject. Any poem, emanating from that type of forced effort, will be discerned as such by any patron reader of the verse. The true poet reflects his feelings, his conscience, and his soul. His techniques bare his innate artistic talents. His sensitivity to his subject matter uncannily evolves from the depth of his soul. He need not know about, or necessarily experience or even research an event for him to be capable of feeling the emotion of the subject matter he may be describing. He is truly a patron of his own artistic ability, just as any other true artist is of his own efforts.

I feel that the poet, (or any person, for that matter) who looks inwardly and who converses with and understands himself, has all the tools necessary to fulfill his desires and to express his genuine emotions.

I further believe that the more a being can communicate and begin to understand and know his inner child, the more easily he will begin to understand himself and all those around him.

Whatever he may do in his life, he has better focus. His insight is keener. Ultimately, he is more relaxed.

I've now begun, this my ninth book, still not believing I have come this far in such a short time. I still go back and read all the other books quite often, enjoying them just as much as when they were first written. Poems are beginning to come my way less frequently lately. I certainly pray that I will be more prolific once again.

I wonder if I will ever catch up with my inner child, let alone myself. In the meantime, enjoy.

Darkman

where am I?

empty dreams limping in the dark

vision voided by walls so blank

a forlorn child sulking in shadows

feeling numbing, touching nothing

where am I?

certainly not where I want to be

open the heart

let the sunlight in

I'll begin with a song

and before not too long

thoughts will gush from my being

and once again I will be singing

Fat Chance Nursery Rhyme Number One

Dipsy doodle, forbidden apple
On my lap sits scrumptious scrapple
One guilty gulp, then weight to grapple
Enter: Dr. Doom's silver scalpel

Heavy, Heavy; What Hangs Over?

during the cold, cold days of winter

under the gray, gray skies a frown

appears on the face of a lonely soul

keeping damp, damp eyes cast down

incessant rain in a sad, sad heart

within a deep, deep thought he found

a future which could be brightened

by casting clear, clear eyes around

The Guidance Counselor

he traversed many moons

and saw galaxies form

and still he knew not

of things which were

about and within him

he loved life

but now his time had come and gone

all the knowledge held

all the queries unanswered

left a sinking heart

thoughts lost forever

like tears in the rain

yet his presence lingers

his memory – rays of sunshine

his love – gentle hands

on my shoulders

his faith – my strength

Catharsis

amoebic cells   anemic swells
conquer the killing bees
tinker bells   triumphant yells
make way for soothing seas

* * * *

So many times great ideas are trapped in the
mind. And sometimes, no matter how hard they try,
they never come out. Sadly, there are some thoughts that
do get out, but are never utilized. How difficult and
frustrating an artist's life can be when he's not creating.

A Busted Melody

one thought
encapsulated in a cell
semen tendril
impatient   persistent
busts out screaming
yearning
dreaming to create a tune
one thought
ends up dying
in some discarded
lost balloon

Of Good Stock

friendly breezes. . . kissing. . . comforting. . . soothing
. . . awakening. . . a thousand and one fingers. . .pleading
    . . . straining to the sky
chattering wings. . . amidst my arms. . . flittering
. . . settling. . . resting. . . in a nested cradle. . . snuggling
    . . . warbling a lullaby
scampering denizens. . . cavorting. . . seeking harbor
. . . feeding. . . solitude. . . savoring the security. . . aloft
    . . . sphered in a majestic high
so strong. . . stand I. . . attached. . . proud
. . . peaceful. . . benevolent. . . cognizant. . . refreshed
    . . . in humble gratitude, I sigh
enthusiasm rampant. . . my toes root for sustenance
. . . life blood pumping. . . to nurture. . . to succor
    . . . as my yearning fingers cry
from a good seed. . . evolved. . . versed, unrehearsed
. . . a melody sublime. . . developing
    . . . enveloping rhapsody
. . . all that I am. . . or ever will be. . . will be I

Fat Chance Nursery Rhyme Number Two

all that's imagined and even more I suppose
is the plight of the man with the pot belly woes
when he peers down the bulb of his rosy red nose
knowing somewhere below lie ten unreachable toes

The Commitment

Crinkles on her forehead. . . . .high spirited

Laughter in her eyes. . . . .flirting fireflies

Hands and feet like ice. . . . .my sacrifice

Enduring tenderness. . . . .sweet sorceress

then she baits me

and she takes me

and she haunts me

and she taunts me

her endeavor

lasts forever

binding tether

ne'er will sever

Dare I heed her? . . . . .yet, I need her

I will hold her. . . . .and behold her

Here beside me. . . . .and inside me

mine forever

one together

all forever

altogether

one forever. . . . .

Dear Child: wait for me

Dear Child:

Some part of me is gone. My writing hand is missing. I feel like the guiding spirit within me has abandoned me and gone on to play with another poet. I feel like I have lost the trail of you, my inner child. I have an awful lot of catching up to do. Where do I begin? What do I do? What can I do?

Dear Child:

May we talk again like we used to do?

I want to see color again. I want to feel the sky and the trees touching me. I want to hear the wind and the flowers speak to me. I want to live in your dreams as I did before. I want to follow your footsteps and call out your name, Your name??! I never knew your name.

Dear Child:

As a butterfly not finding nectar, I am flitting aimlessly from one thing to another. The clangor of my steel wings is driving me crazy. Have you gone inside the cardinal outside my window? Day in, day out, he bangs his head against my window panes. I was always led to believe that his specie is a territorial twit trying to protect his turf. Maybe he is really trying to get back inside. Is that true? We are both banging our heads against the wall. How do I get to you? I am going to have to ponder that for a bit.

Dear Child: wait for me

Breakout

stand clear

let my heart break out

and shout

let no fear

stifle it's right to be

totally free

to savor the day

and fly

lifted by wings of love

beyond the above

buoyed by winds of trust

escape I must

I shout

my heart breaks out

I have no fear

so stand clear

Flashpoint

the burning desire to lounge by the fire

with dancing flames playing mind spin games

sets thoughts to lapse, and a dream perhaps

flits from the ash as a brilliant mind flash

a heart is uplifted, a conscience feels gifted

the creativity of the night horizons the light

Tee Tantrum

To take the time to thaw ten throbbing toes

Try twisting these thrice then titillate those

Thinking this therapy throttles the throes

'Tis tactless text touting tainted tableaus

Instant Recall

I walk within the forest, exhilarated with the lush
My senses, although keen, are mesmerized by the hush
The lack of any sound at all takes my breath away
I feel as if there is no time and forever is today
My mind is purged of clutter, my heart is dancing free
I find no other space in life where I would rather be
Tranquility within is a tonic at my beck and call
When I do return to sounds so common to us all

Catching Up

do I know you?
up from the depths of me
do I know you?
I am yours for me to see
up from the roots
up into the tree
up thru the limbs
to the sky and the free
over the mountain
over the sea
follow the wind song
following me
I am behind you
stay nearby me
I am beside you
now we are free

Timedrops

borrowed time

borrowed drops

a life fulfilled

time stops

I walk through the woods

stepping the trail softly

the sky is bawling

drops are falling

thru the canopy

life's panoply

in time

I capture the drops

sated leaf's release

accepted in peace

borrowed time

borrowed drops

Once Upon a Rocking Horse

Once upon a rocking horse,
A fair lad rode into dream
There was no land that was too far,
No star beyond his gleam,
He rode thru time and history,
Winning battles, conquering foes
A knight in shining armor he
From his plumage to his toes
He rode that night the British came,
Revere running by his side
Low in saddle in Churchill Downs
Matching Seabiscuit stride for stride
Tall in the saddle in Tombstone town,
A badge upon his vest
Protecting all the townsfolk from the Kid,
The Daltons and all the rest
The faster he rocked, the farther he rode,
Pegasus became his steed
He was the master of all the galaxies
Even Andromeda agreed
His Father's call, his Mother's plea
Returned him to caring side
His quests would wait for another time
When he went for another ride

There is no End . . . . . . Only a Beginning

Each new day brings a new dawn

Each new sunset sets anticipation for that new day

Each sleep seeks a new dream

Each raindrop comes from a new direction

Hits a new place . . . . . wets a new space

Each life brings a new life

Each new bud springs a new bloom

Each person met is a new friend found

Each of us is unique

We strive in parallel

Move congruently . . . . . live concurrently

We are peace . . . . . not turmoil

We are love . . . . . not hate

We are the beginning . . not the end . . for there is no end

Raging Bull

Flittering fluttering, free formed fun
whatever became of the frivolous one?
fear in his fingers, afraid of the sun
alone as the night, his pain has begun
His time is now over, his day is now done
Clown in his pocket, a man on the run
Tickles his fancy, his hand on his gun
Free as the wind, his battle's now won

August Valentine

Woven strands of dewy silver glisten
When a bright summer's dawn comes peeping thru
Yet just before like shrouds on a specter
Draped the dark shadows with a dismal hue
How quickly can a sad moment brighten
When a smile from the heart says "I love you"

So Say You

So say you of gentler ways
Who during your quiet hours
Belays the times of wonder days
To smell the lesser flowers

Scribbles and Doodles

I'm composing these lines from scratch
but here's the troublesome rub
an itch to write remains just an itch
when words don't flow, that's a bitch

* * * *

'tis but a stroke of genius when
a verse just flows from a poet's pen

* * * *

I stand toasting the hale and the hearty
with just gestures at the writers' block party

* * * *

Heed the poet's battle cry
"the word is out, well versed am I"

* * * *

I'm a little older now
perhaps wiser at this age
I'm a little older now
I've turned another page
I'm a little older now
nothing rhymes with sixty
So for me to get this ditty done
I'll have to wait for sixty one

Towards Saving Precious Moments

silent songs
whispering in the air
undertones of tenuous dread
I've aged a year, and yet
thoughts are young
still free
still fresh
still me
the meadows of the mind
still swaying
still gently receiving my body lain
my nostrils still sense the golden grain
and my eyes receive all the reverie
how can that be?
songs long lost
no longer sought
lying within
spin to my edge of thought
silent songs
whispering in the air
silent tones
yawning away the blues
I stretch awake the sun
looking forward
to yet more vibrant hues

My Hero

Captain Nemo, my hearty helmsman
yester-pilot from a future time
dove the chambered Nautilus
down through the inky brine

Captain Nemo, my hallowed helmsman
twenty thousand leagues beyond his peers
tamed the depths unchartered
while conquering all his fears

Captain Nemo, my hearty hero
my helmsman of fictional fame
who rode the pages of history
sending imaginations to flame

My God! Where do I go from here?

My universe is as large or as small as I want it to be. How much imagination can I muster? Am I a part of a larger tree or are there other trees growing within me?

I wonder how many others have dreamed thoughts like me. Sometimes I feel myself getting smaller and smaller until I'm conversing with the cells of my body; and then I get even smaller. The views of this inner space are so vast just like the universe of outer space. During the same sequence of thoughts, I feel myself getting larger and larger until the whole universe of outer space appears so small and it seems just like the cells I had been conversing with and experiencing earlier.

If the make-up of an atom, the building blocks of life, is to my body what a solar system is to the whole universe, then I am, in some ways, a universe of my own. That is fascinating.

The possibilities for discussion are endless. Perhaps when I die (or pass on), I am passing from one universe into another. Maybe I am born again, reincarnated into some other being, some other universe. Then, I am something in a sometime world, somewhere.

My God! Where do I go from here?

Penmanship

While away the hours in passing
    fleet of foot,
    don't tarry
    don't stray
    thoughts pondered, not written
    run with the deer
    run with the wind
    disappear

While away the hours in muse
    great thoughts savored
    marveled in mind
    gone wherever
    lost forever
    in the land of ever

While away the hours ecstatic
    a penman wrote
        of dreams
        of golden ships on silvery seas
        of morning dews, of loves and tears
        of mountains high, of stately trees
        of hours turned into wonder years

While away the hours remembered
    through the stampede of fleeting time
    though the eye who reads will ne'er forget
    the penman or his everlasting rhyme

Bounding Verse

Lured by a waving mist
Swallowed by a raving sea
Dashed on singing rocks and slithering
Smashed into bubbling foam and withering
Flowing in, flowing out of me

* * * *

My Cache

Open, oh my Sesame, open
my seeds of thought encased
what treasures lie within
what will salivate my taste
Open, oh my Sesame, open
a shell within my hardened shell
what do I need to crack the casing
so within me, you no longer dwell
Open, oh my Sesame, open
have I no quest, no rhyme, no reason
dare I challenge, dare I blossom
if not my inner self screams "treason"
Open, oh my Sesame, open
let me grasp within, your giving hand
stay, oh, creative heartfelt touch
may all be golden gems, not driven sand
Open, oh my Sesame. open
set my mind and heart at ease
what is learned best be not forgotten
golden blooms my precious soul foresees

Here I am again

here I am again
no impressions, no expressions, no feelings
another beautiful fall day of splendor
burnished leaves falling down
squirrels and chipmunks going nuts over nuts
but that's just it
nothing else
no inspirations, no aspirations, no revelations
nothing challenges the mind
nothing excites the fingers
only the emptiness lingers
so here I am again
in the doldrums
out of touch with my soul
I must reach out to the depths of me
perhaps go hug a tree
lie down in the grass
cavort with the leaves
let nature take me on a discovery spree
or do I merely once again talk with Thee
here I am again
and here I go

Not a Mis-gnomer

A crack of thunder and a lone star gnome of wonder
        rode screaming in on his bronco's pride
With gollypogghs blinking
        and the ellywumpphs drinking
        gnome just sat there smug and all wise-eyed
Silly snipperwhapps snickered
        while whimditties dickered
        each claiming they had nothing dear to hide
But gnome, knowing better, composed a quickie letter
        claiming common sense as the sole bonafide
Snipperwhapps began flinging
        as whimditties began winging
        mood mudpies that each
                were generously supplied
Gnome basked in virtual glory,
        retelling the same old story
        wiggling ears and calmly standing wide
Snipperwhapps were hobnobbing;
        whimditties were sob-sobbing
        that it was time that new diapers be applied
Gollypogghs and ellywhumpps
        off their couch potato rumps
        overwhelmingly let whimditties step aside
Now regal snipperwhapps
        evolving from phoenix razorbapps
        vowed tipperees and hillaries
        would never be denied
And the lone star gnome of wonder in a crack of thunder
                rode out knowing that he had really tried

Changes

on the edge of my life
courses unset, a shadow emerges
coming from some other medium
some other time
what brings myself to greet
this other side
alter ego, not withstanding
I accept the change
the crisis of a journey
while on holiday to this time
is but one golden leaf
upon the forest floor
my shadow within
sensing this time before time
fondles the leaf, and
as if coming from some other medium
emerges from my teardrops
fluttering away to the edge of some other time

Through the eyes of a loving God

He who has vanquished the tests of his time
He who can relish some wit and some rhyme
He who believes in himself and his life
He who has withstood adversity and strife
He who through compassion and love sets his course
He who knows truly that there's a powerful force
He is an achiever, a martyr, a man for all seasons
He is a king of his peers and a slave to his legions
He remains humble and in this strength he survives
He will live on forever in everyone's lives

On Shaking Hands with the Sun

deep in slumber dark, lost unto the world

rapt in fantasy. . . . . . . mind in cozy curled

light crept in over edge of comfort thread

leaving all my dreams, tucked away in bed

fancies still remain. . . . . . vividly and wild

conversations held. . . . with my inner child

ecstasy salivating. . . . . lingering into dawn

recall of reveries soothing. . . . . . then gone

awake, awake, rush headstrong into light

a day to make, so taste the morning bright

dewdrops on the lips. . . nectar in my heart

spring up on dancing feet, depart, depart

Upbeat

no good

say what?

it's just no good

so tell me about it already

it's no good to see the moth thus so

flittering and fluttering here as tho'

it was trying to grasp the mystic light

spiraling dizzily in a frenzied flight

if he does reach the light and yes, no doubt

he'll be frazzled and frayed and all burned out

you are right   no good

it's no good of you to think thus so

that moth has a reason; so let him go

if you had a goal and had it clearly in sight

you'd soar to achieve it, no matter the height

so say to you now; rise up and move out

desires will be triumphs, of that I've no doubt

The Aura of the Mystic Ouija: Circa 1946

Master of words
Chairman of the board
Knowing all
Seeing all
Feeling all
Telling all
Waits
Static
Anticipating
Two siblings facing one another
Brother's knees touch sister's
Board on laps
Backs straight
Sixteen fingers hover
Thumbs askew
Barely touching the Mystic
Question posed
Answers sought
Two minds
Concentrating as one
Ecstatic
Ouija begins to move
Slowly
Unhesitatingly
Deliberately
Then swiftly
With authority
Puppet fingers following
Barely keeping up
A question is answered
Letter by letter
Word by word
Mystical silence   (continues)

Awesome wisdom
Incredible!!
"You did it!!!"
"No! You did it!!"
Scintillating thrill
Mystery still.

An Entry into Prose Number Six: The Tryst

I stand in the forest as I so often do; for I love the solitude. I love its greeting and our meeting.

Through the forest haze I listened and I heard the whisper of dawn. In the reflective still of a pool, my eyes gazed into the eyes of a brave who surely I should remember. We shed the same tears and watched the same rivers flow.

Our moccasins are threadbare having traveled all this time. The hemlocks, as is with all that is around us, seem ancient, yet as fresh as the day's rising. His bowstring is not flexed, - limp; the arrow's fletching is frayed and misshapen and the tips not as sharp as they once were.

As one, we knelt, touching the moist earth, feeling yesterday and tomorrow. Words were non existent. Thoughts stampeded through the forest quiet and echoed serenely back to mind. There are no footfalls left in our wake only those before us going on and out of sight.

I stand as part of the Whole and of the All.
Something wonderful this way comes.

Wisdom is breathing down my neck and tingling
sensitive skin. We stand in awe of only one
magnificence, that of the Great Alone.
We are the All and the Forever is now.
I stand strong.
Destiny is staring me straight in the eye.
I stand as my forefathers and all those fathers to be
Forever with the Great Alone.
Forever as one.

To Rue or Not to Rue

Regret
Don't fret
Forget
No sweat

Bloomin' Lethargy

Don't just ponder
the yonder bluet
Get up, and
wander over to it

Enter the Budding Herald

Bubbling and babbling, gurgling thru the carefree kiddy kill
Squiggling and wiggling and giggling o'er the rocky rising rill
I am a buoyant buttercup bouncing, - bobbing with the flow
I'm going where 'ere it takes me; my heart's a cheerful glow
I feel all the exhilaration blossoming and tickling deep inside
Happiness, like a sweet caress, takes me on this waterslide
Squiggling and wiggling and giggling o'er the rocky riant rill
Bubbling and babbling, gurgling thru the carefree kiddy kill

A Trilogy: Pebbles, Ponds and Parables

The Pebbles: Rocks of Ages

river stones. . . . . history gatherers
water wizened. . . . . laying by the river's edge
sleeping smoothly. . . . . honed silently
oiled by crystal elixirs. . . . . never done
. . . . lay shimmering in the sun
river stones. . . . . talc like, soft serenes
. . . . . . moved only by stronger means
river stones. . . . . . . lonesome, yet oh so grand
. . . . in time, like man, turned back to sand

The Ponds: Thru a Looking Glass

breathless, depthless, peaceful, reflective
an eye to the sky. . . . . . . a peep to the deep
a ripple run. . . . . .spun from a breach
in surface tension holds a lifelong pension
to remain so stoic,   so lonesome, so alive
to thrive. . . . . replenish. . . . . and to survive

The Parables: Lore

Doom loomed in endless gloom

Every nook and cranny, every room

The dark, the dank the deathly still

Stood like ghosts from a warring kill

What had been said atop a tower of dread

Was that a raconteur,

a desolate derelict draped in thread

slumping in dark shadows

mumbling tattered tales

spinning anemic yarns

speaking over countless years to absent ears

Cherubs of hope with twinkling lights

chased the shadows from the heights

The loom awoke and spun golden dreams

spreading words past the tower's beams

Enlightened verse danced with the sun

the day of telling had again begun

The words emanated around and about

Trees whispered down the valley

Fish jumped over silver rainbows

Wings of song soared skyward

Sending alpine echoes to the near and far horizon

All hearts were young and gay, so they say

So the tale unfolds. So the legend goes.

The Poet's Arena

GAME ONE
wait and write what comes so naturally
just like the rising sun
an itchy crotch to push a silent pen
ends just where you've begun

GAME TWO
most of the hamstrung hours
inspiration sulks and cowers
the rarest unknown hours
produce the morning flowers

GAME THREE
If you let your intellect get overbooked
Your imagination may get overlooked

GAME FOUR
his bane, stay sane, don't feign
    hesitate
talk plain, big gain, champagne
    celebrate

Suckers

he fed his line
casting no doubt
and by design
the thread spun out
a patient wait
thru discipline
they took the bait
he reeled them in

A Natural Sketch

Guided by an unseen brush held hand
Billowy puffs finger-walked the land
Shadow painting seas of swaying grain
Casting tones across the vast terrain

I've done some Japanese haiku before; however, this is my first attempt at a Tanka. The first three lines are the same as a haiku: five syllables, then seven syllables and thirdly, five syllables. Unlike the haiku, which leaves the reader with his own thoughts to complete the poem; the Tanka concludes the thought in two more lines each containing seven syllables.

Toys

toys in the attic
laying dusted in darkness
buried deep in dreams
toys for boys' creative games
swept aside by growing pains

* * * *

Night-watch

shadow stalks the moonlit corn
as all of the furrows wealth
stretches up to grasp the night
and eliminate the stealth
darkness strikes in fierce reprise
to squelch the growth so fragile
instinctive urge to rise and purge
the incessant nightly frazzle

Star-doom

A star died for me today

iota became a nova

alpha became omega

I see the past before me

instant radiant glory

a dying star

explodes into the future

in my time, greeting me

enveloping me

my thoughts span the distance

starlight spans the time

and yet, now 'tis gone

and life must carry on

Poetry Today

The poetry that is written in our world today; what is it? What should it be? When it comes to poetry, I am not a purist for I write my feelings as they flow. I may be a considered a contemporary or renaissance writer. I don't wedge the thoughts into the format of a sonnet or sestina or whatever the masters of the past used as their formats for their expressions. I can see a studious poet drilling himself to learn and understand the ways of old but it should remain as that, an exercise. His own feelings are far from just a series of exercises.

To me, poetry today is extemporaneous and needs no format. Rhyme may intermingle with blank or free verse or may not appear at all. What I like or dislike is my taste and is initially written for my eyes only. I cannot nor should not criticize someone else's expressions of his feelings. However, I can criticize his choice of presentation. Let me explain.

When a writer's intellect takes over, name-droppings, archaic word groupings and past poets' techniques are implemented. The poet, in my opinion, has missed the boat. Sing-song rhyme becomes trite and the impact of an excellent theme could be demoralized. The poet does not let his innovation, his imagination or his creativity run free. He becomes a slave to a set rhyme or an academic structure. He has manufactured a poem rather than create it. The wind that blows beneath the stars and the wind that whistles through a tunnel require two different feelings and probably two different poetic thoughts.

Upon My Soul

I held my heart in my hand
And watched and felt it jump
And when I stuffed it back inside
I realized it was just a pump
Where then do I get my feelings
What really comes from above
It's more than moving blood refreshed
It's more than compassion and love
All my dreams, my wishes, all of my desires
All my thoughts converge to form my whole
All of my emotions all do inspire me
To fulfill and nourish my heart and soul
But it's my soul that is the master of my craft
If it's my desire to win, to dare, to innovate
To take my natural talents to their limits
Let my mind create no boundaries for that state

Blizzard of '93

On this day a 'once in a lifetime' blizzard rages outside.
We have a white-out.
I sit here warmly hovelled and am keyboarding my
thoughts to screen and relishing the play

> My dear wife worries over all the 'What ifs?"
>
> What if the electricity goes off?
>
> What if we have no heat" do we have any wood?
>
> What if no lights? Get the candles, flashlights?
>
> What if? What if?
>
> My thoughts reflect on the "Why nots?"
>
> Why not sit back, relax and enjoy it?
>
> Why not to worry?
>
> Why not revel in nature's wrath and fun?
>
> Why not? Why not?

I am excited for this day.
Why not relax?
What if you did?

Life's Play

Statuesque silhouette standing still
      against a leering moon
Don't be afraid; don't begin to swoon
Tiny silvery sparkling needles
      surround the silent specter
Dare we sip the elusive luring nectar?
The play resumes in three befalling acts
      of awesome splendor
Enraptured, we are drawn and torn asunder
Taken from the lightless caves of lurking loveless fright
To the soaring spires of spiraling delight
Taken from the shivering cellars
      of a sunken sodden sorrow
To the laughing mirrors of a bright tomorrow
This final act is a baffling brutal scene
      we've come to share
Tragedy and Comedy mimic one another's stare.
Which true mask is borne upon that cryptic
      silhouetted face
Show yourself!   To whom do we embrace?
If we could glimpse beyond the mask
      before this play is though
We hope it would be a face that is becoming you

My Own Video Game

Without leaving my seat………or moving not a muscle
I can walk and I can talk…………with a tiny corpuscle
I can journey to the near……...and far ends of the earth
I can witness the miracle………..of the Bethlehem birth
I can swim in every ocean….or can climb up every tree
I can burn upon a stake………or be the stinger of a bee
I can be the bough that breaks .....or bade the cradle fall
I can move mighty mountains, or do nothing much at all
I can be the sweet essence…...of a rambling yellow rose
I can be the nylon fiber……...on a leg of someone's hose
I can be a mighty knight ……..at Arthur's big roundtable
I can be his horse of white….eating oats out in his stable
I can be a universe……..spinning circles far out in space
I can be tiny raindrops splashing on your upturned face
I can be a sharpened pencil……..writing a lovely sonnet
I can be an Easter bonnet………with all the frills upon it
I can be a cathedral……...with music ringing in my nave
I can be a sinking sailing ship………or I can be the wave
I can be the wind blown freely or be penned up in a cell
I can be the red apple atop the son's head of William Tell
I can be any master villain…..and give them each a name
Without lifting any finger……….I can destroy their fame
I can be almost anything…………..I can think myself to do
Oops, there is one tiny thing………....I can not be like you

One of these days

I'm gonna getcha
you betcha
and when I finally do
I'll have forgotten
all the rotten
things you used to do

Songs of Your Life

I

take you to the seaside waters
to the rim of pounding surf
let your toes and nimble fingers
feel the edge of nature's birth
let you breathe the spray of sunshine
let you walk the sand and turf
if you're here to just remember
let the sea renew your worth

II

in the silence of the forest
in the pools of mystic thoughts
in the depths of liquid treasures
in the rush of heartfelt soughts
go and seek what is before you
catch your soul before it falls
go you forth and wander freely
hark the hush, your spirit calls

III

in the essence of a rosebud
in the midst of crimson fire
lie the seeds of truth and wisdom
encased in petals of desire
as the sunlight greets the blossom
so the soul greets peace within
all the love embraces freedom
accept His love, let life begin

The Flame

the candle's strong, the candle's bright

the candle's snuffed of living light

like shifting sands upon the shore

time brings change forevermore

tho' sands be changed by swirling seas

no one can change the memories

as a light burns on in a musing mind

a soul is treasured like a miner's find

tho' the flame soars out of living sight

the candle's strong, the candle's bright

Come Here and Look

the murmuring of the softly falling rain
though the idyllic friendly hours abate
this captured melody must in mind remain
oh, to wallow in this hypnotic state
come here and look, I hope it's not too late

crystal tears slide down my window pane
and watercolors from the artist's plate
evolves into my surrealistic domain
oh, to wallow in this hypnotic state
come here and look, I hope it's not too late

through prisms, I view tomorrow's ordain
as the sun may change the painting's fate
my mind sets out to supplant and ingrain
oh to wallow in this hypnotic state
come here and look, I hope it's not too late

Trochee One

Hustle, hustle, stay your bustle

Tussle, tussle, lots of muscle

Trochee Two

Rattle, rattle, viper's prattle

Danger signal, seek no battle

Long   Gone   Song

heartfelt songs scamper softly skyward

follow the rhythm or wait for the echo

yet the song may never return

no. the song may never return

just follow the rhythm to a lofty peak

catch the song before it goes off beat

or the song may never return

no, the song may never return

Out on a Limb

Too the far reaches he wanders and searches

Out on a limb on a blossom he perches

So far from the earth, so nimble his carry

To the ends of his world, bearing his quarry

So far from his farm, will he find his way home?

An adventuresome soul, all alone does he roam

What has a sassafras bloom within it to savor

To an ant on a limb, it has an elegant flavor

Out on a limb on a blossom he perches

To the far reaches he wanders and searches

Poet's Lament

To take a tune from Simon's boon
Long time lasting
A classic thought can be brought
Here, here to stay
One sad thought drenched in fraught
Long time weeping
A wretched heart may soon depart
Far, far away
Where have all the poems gone?
Long time passing
Where have all the poems gone?
Far, far away
I ache to sing an old mindsong
Long time yearning
No new thoughts to me belong
Gone, gone away
Bones are old, the child is old
Long time chasing
Though I'll bet, I'll catch up yet
Ne'er, ne'er today
Sky is bright, come see the light
Long time burning
The child is near, the child is here
Kneel, kneel and pray

From the Notebook: The Chase is on

The chase is on. All is alive and well again. New fervor
has spurred the heart and mind to seek and find the soul
of my youth. To rise from the fuzzy realm of this present
existence is testimony to that renewed fervor. The child
is here and waiting. I need to be patient and need to
know when I have reached his presence. Being there and
not knowing you have arrived is experience all too
familiar to me. I cannot let this opportunity pass me by
again.

The chase is on

Plant the seed
Follow your lead
Clear of mind
Seek
Find
The chase is on
Hold your breath
Go with the stars
With the wind
Seek
Find
The chase is on
Fleet of foot
Stay the course
Lag not behind
Seek
Find

After Word:

Something has been brought to mind which requires me to clarify and justify my input pertaining to the quality of my literary journey of thoughts.

My poetry writing has been like a lifework or a life's work of effort. I wrote each entry in chronological order and omitted nothing. Under-par work was never deleted. Every human being's life carries baggage along with the good wishes. My published books and ready manuscripts reflect that aspect. If I had deleted anything that I thought to be imperfect; I feel that all of the same genre of thoughts would have appeared to look false; - and maybe even boring. As they say - "Variety is the spice of life." So as it is within my true life's journal; my original intent prevails. I hope you understand and appreciate my position.

However, at this time I do have a confession to make. I left out an entire portion of my life. In that particular time of my life; I had the time of my life. I wrote, and have yet to publish, another book entitled: *The Good Times Party Songbook: just about one hundred and thirty one remembered, forgotten & ill-begotten drinking ditties, bawdy ballads, giddy gaudy games, lewdy tunes and murdered melodies.* This book has only lyrics, and subject matter ranges from mild to extreme. Some is not for the faint of heart. Purchasing and reading same would be discretionary and certainly at your own "risqué."

(continues)

The following edited excerpt is from the aforementioned manuscript's epilogue:

"The events foretold and all the different types of songs sung began for me, beginning in the summer of 1944. The Second World War was almost over. I was twelve years old and it was my first year at Boy Scout summer camp. Singing songs was a big part of having fun, for we sang them after breakfast, lunch and dinner in the dining hall. We also sang at the campfire ceremonies which were twice a week. I spent eight years, six as a camper and two as a merit badge counselor on the camp staff and also as the Camp Waterfront Director. The camp staff also had the chance to lead the singing.

By 1946 the war was over, and the happiness was seen in all the smiling faces, and in a healthy society with a solid sense of morality. These were the good times. Songs and singing them was a natural thing during this happy time. You could hear it and feel it. Naturally and fortunately, for me, college followed; as well as the opportunity to do more singing. So it was a continuation of song; however, the content and humor changed in how and what was sung. But I never forgot my early years and incorporated past and present in my ever-growing repertoire.

Singing became important during my years in the United States Navy, my hometown social gang party years, and with my sons through their times as scouts. Also being a scoutmaster for ten more years of summer camp fun (same camp) and finally running Penn State bus trips to football games for 27 years.

Believe it or not, I am still sporadically singing to this day at fun things during my retirement years. That adds up to sixty five fun-packed, song-filled wonderful years. My wife, Shirley, had to bear it all. God Bless Shirley!

The total merriment and experiences gleaned from all those years have made it a pleasure to put this book together. Please excuse some of the language and thoughts but that is the baggage and sometimes the garbage that goes with the flow of life."

The Beginning. . . . . .

Seek

Find